Christmas at Long Pond

by **William T. George**

paintings by **Lindsay Barrett George**

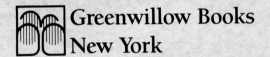

Greenwillow Books
New York

Special thanks to William Speare, Curator of Science
at the Everhart Museum, Scranton, Pennsylvania
—L. B. G.

Gouache paints were used for the full-color art.
The text type is ITC Berkeley Old Style Bold.

Library of Congress
Cataloging-in-Publication Data
George, William T.
    Christmas at Long Pond/by William T. George ;
paintings by Lindsay Barrett George.
        p.   cm.
    Summary: Father and son observe the plant
and animal life around Long Pond before
finding just the right Christmas tree.
    ISBN 0-688-09214-4.
    ISBN 0-688-09215-2 (lib. bdg.)
    [1. Nature—Fiction.   2. Winter—Fiction.
3. Fathers and sons—Fiction.
4. Christmas—Fiction.]
I. George, Lindsay Barrett, ill.   II. Title.
PZ7.G29344Ch   1992   [Fic]—dc20
91-31475   CIP   AC

FOR SUSAN

In the quiet darkness before dawn, a snowshoe hare softly nibbles twigs from a fallen poplar branch.
S W O O O S H ! ! !
The great horned owl's talons barely miss their prey. Desperate and hungry, the owl wheels and tries to follow. The hare escapes through a tangled thicket of mountain laurel and safely reaches his bed.

The owl perches on the branch of a pine tree and waits. But the hunt is over. The rays of the sun blink through a tree on the far side of Long Pond. Another winter's day has begun.

A doe and her two fawns
sleep under a young
hemlock tree.
It is still too cold to move.
The deer wait until the
morning chill is gone.
The fawns rise from their
beds and follow their
mother in search of food.

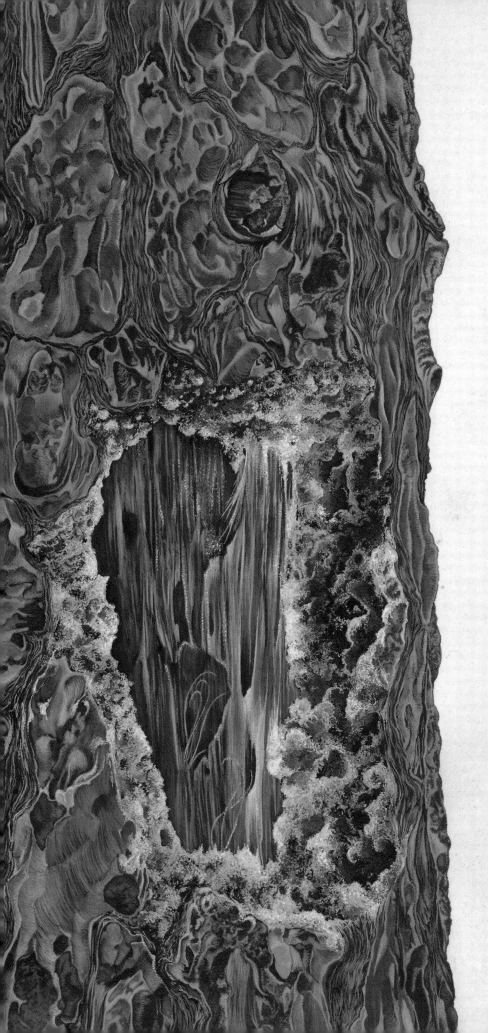

KNOCK! KNOCK!
KNOCK! KNOCK!
A piliated woodpecker's
loud taps shatter the
morning's peace. Splinters
shower down the trunk of
a white pine tree. The
woodpecker is searching
for carpenter ants. During
the warmer months, the
woodpecker flew from tree
to tree listening for ants
moving in their hidden
tunnels. He pecked wedge-
shaped holes into the
ants' nests.

Now the sleeping ants
make no sound, but the
holes cut during the
summer mark those trees
where they can be found.

The woodpecker is too busy to notice his audience below.

The father and son continue on their way, past birch trees
and lilac bushes and the fallen stones of an old farm wall.
"Are we almost there?" the little boy asks.
"The field is just a little farther," answers his father.
"Can I choose the tree?" asks the boy.
"Yes, of course," says his father.

They finally reach the old field.
"How about this one, Dad? It's a beauty."
"Looks perfect. Can you hold this branch back?
  Your grandfather planted these spruce trees," he says.
"Most of them are too big now, but they make good cover
  for the deer and birds when the weather gets bad."

The spruce tree is cut and lashed
to the toboggan. The father looks up
at the afternoon sun.
"See if you can find the way back," he says.
With his eyes on the ground, the boy
retraces their footprints
through the snow.

The small caravan reaches the old stone wall. The father
stops and whistles softly, twice. The boy looks up and
sees three deer standing under an old apple tree.
No one moves. Finally the doe snorts and leaps away,
flashing her white tail. The two fawns follow.
"The deer moved first," whispers the boy.
"Yes, they did," said his father. "You were very good.
You were as quiet as a mouse."

Father and son push on, backtracking
through the woods. They come upon fox prints.
The prints were not there this morning.

The father stops again, within sight of Long Pond.
"I'm going to cut down a poplar tree," he says. "I want
you to sit on that big stone over there. This tree will
not reach that far."
"Should I hold Sam?" asks the boy.
"Yes," answers his father. "You can never be sure which
way a tree will fall, and I don't want either of you
to get hurt."
He unlashes an ax and a bucksaw from the toboggan.
He cuts a notch in the tree with the ax.

Then he saws toward the top of the notch from the other side of the tree. Before he cuts all the way through, the tree leans forward, picks up speed, and crashes into the snow. Branches snap and break.

"Now the deer will have plenty to eat," he tells his son. "When you cut down a poplar in the winter, the roots send up saplings in the spring. Not just by the stump, like most trees, but everywhere above the roots."

Father and son slide the toboggan onto Long Pond. The sun has set behind the hill. They start to walk across the frozen pond. It begins to snow.

They kneel beside the beaver lodge. The father picks
up a stick that the beavers have gnawed smooth.
"Try this," he says. "Put one end against the lodge,
and carefully touch your ear to the other end."
The boy's eyes widen. "It works!" he says. "Somebody's
home. I can hear them moving around."
"I can't hear anything but the snow falling," says the father.
"We'd better get home if we're going to get this tree trimmed.
It's getting dark, and tomorrow is Christmas!"